The Cat Who Smelled Like Cabbage

Other books in this series:
The Dog Who Loved to Race
The Hamster Who Got Himself Stuck
The Parrot Who Talked Too Much

Unless otherwise indicated, all Scripture references are from the Good News Bible, copyright American Bible Society, 1976.

Cover design by Durand Demlow
Illustrations by Anne Gavitt

THE CAT WHO SMELLED LIKE CABBAGE
© 1990 by Neta Jackson
Published by Multnomah Press
10209 SE Division Street
Portland, Oregon 97266

Multnomah Press is a ministry of Multnomah School of the Bible, 8435 NE Glisan Street, Portland, Oregon 97220.

Printed in Singapore.

Library of Congress Cataloging-in-Publication Data

Jackson, Neta.
    The cat who smelled like cabbage / Neta Jackson.
        p. cm. —(Pet parables)
        Summary: Although Siamese Cat is prejudiced against Alley Cat because of her ugly appearance and unconventional behavior, Black Cat makes up her own mind and finds Alley Cat to be a gentle and kind friend. Includes a Bible verse and discussion questions.
    ISBN 0-88070-349-0
    [1. Cats—Fiction. 2. Prejudices—Fiction. 3. Parables.]
I. Series: Jackson, Neta. Pet parables.
PZ7.J13684Cat   1990
[E]—dc20   90-48382
                                                                            CIP
                                                                            AC

91 92 93 94 95 96 97 98 99 - 10 9 8 7 6 5 4 3 2 1

The Cat Who Smelled Like Cabbage

Neta Jackson

Illustrated by Anne Gavitt

MULTNOMAH

Portland, Oregon 97266

Black Cat stretched her hind legs wa-a-y back, sniffed the morning air with her button nose, then trotted briskly down the sidewalk. She turned in at the house next door, where her friend Siamese Cat was warming herself in a sunny spot on the porch railing.

"Why, hello, Black Cat," she said, as Black Cat bounded up the porch steps. "Whatever are you so energetic for?" Siamese Cat took a couple of long licks of her neck fur.

"Because it's a beautiful day!" exclaimed Black Cat, bounding up onto the railing beside her friend.

"It's a horrible day. Can't you smell the cabbage cooking across the street?" Another couple of licks with her dainty tongue. "But then, I suppose you don't have a nose as sensitive as mine. Mixed breeds never do."

Black Cat looked sideways at Siamese Cat and sighed. "No, I suppose not. There are times I wish I knew what sort of family my father came from, but. . . ."

Siamese Cat purred soothingly. "There, there, don't worry about it. You are beautiful, just the same. Why, your blue-black fur and white feet are quite exquisite, really. And you belong to nice People, and I don't hold it against you that he is a Small Businessman instead of a Doctor like my People. Not at all."

Black Cat started to say something, but Siamese Cat suddenly stiffened. Black Cat looked across the street and saw a large awkward gray cat (or was it brownish? or spotted?) ambling up the walk of the house with the cabbage smell.

"You can be glad you aren't Alley Cat over there," sniffed Siamese Cat disdainfully. "Now there is somebody you shouldn't associate with."

Black Cat nodded, and hardly realized that she said, "Why?"

"Why! Because, that's why. She lives across the street, for one thing. For another thing, she doesn't really live there—I mean, she doesn't really belong to anyone. They just give her scraps now and then."

Black Cat thought of her bowl of Golden Nugget Cat Food every morning.

"Besides," Siamese Cat went on, beginning to lick her milky-brown fur again, "she is so ugly. There's not a graceful bone in her body—lack of good breeding, of course."

Black Cat began licking her own soft fur, grateful that she was not ugly like Alley Cat.

"But the worst thing of all," Siamese Cat suddenly hissed, with her eyes narrowed and her tail swishing emphatically, "is. . . ."

"Is what?" Black Cat said, stopping her tongue in mid-lick and looking at her friend with wide eyes.

". . . the way she roams around the neighborhood at night while decent cats like us are in bed where they should be. Disgraceful."

Siamese Cat finished her bath in silence. Then, "Well, enough of that. I forgot to ask how your children are."

"Children!" Black Cat exclaimed. "Oh, I'm glad you reminded me. They are getting so rambunctious that if I don't hurry back home, they will be tumbling out of the box and getting into everything. I really must hurry along." She jumped off the porch railing with one graceful movement and hurried down the steps. "Oh, shall we go for our walk as usual this afternoon?" she called back over her shoulder.

"Of course, Dearie," Siamese Cat purred. As Black Cat trotted away, Siamese Cat sighed. "Children. What a bother they are. I'm glad they're hers and not mine."

Black Cat's kittens fussed over their lunch, socked and played with each other, and just would not settle down. Finally, they seemed to drop off to sleep for their nap out of plain tiredness.

Black Cat sighed. "They really are good children," she thought fondly, "but how do I get them to settle down for their naps properly after lunch?" She took one last look, and padded softly out of the house so she wouldn't be late for her walk with Siamese Cat.

"I would ask Siamese Cat for advice," she thought as she headed down the sidewalk, "but I know just what she'd say. 'That's your problem, Dearie!' "

Just then Black Cat thought she heard a familiar sound, a tiny mew. Then everything happened so quickly—the blast of a car horn, a tiny blur in the street, a large gray body streaking past her. And just as quickly it was all over, and there was Alley Cat gently dropping one of Black Cat's kittens at her feet.

"What happened?" Black Cat gasped. She anxiously licked her kitten all over. It didn't seem to be hurt.

"I'm not sure," Alley Cat said shyly. "I think your little kitten followed you out of the house. When I saw it toddling into the street . . . well, I didn't wait to find out if you knew about it or not."

"Oh. Well, thank you very much." Black Cat was beginning to feel uncomfortable. Up close, Alley Cat really was ugly. Her left ear was ragged, and her body seemed full of lumps. And she wasn't gray at all, but black and yellow and brown and white. Black Cat had to admit that Alley Cat wasn't exactly dirty, but she definitely smelled like cabbage.

"Black Cat!" It was Siamese Cat calling from her porch-railing throne. "Whatever are you doing? You are late for our walk!"

"Oh, I guess I must be going," Black Cat said hurriedly. "Uh—but I do want to thank you for coming to the rescue of my kitten. Really I do."

"I'm glad it's not hurt," Alley Cat said softly. "You see, I have kittens, too."

Black Cat stopped in her tracks and blinked in surprise. "You do?"

"Oh, yes," Alley Cat smiled shyly. "Eight of them, and they're almost four weeks old!"

"But . . ." Black Cat seemed embarrassed, but her curiosity got the best of her. "But . . . where do you live? I mean, where do you keep your kittens?"

"In the bushes behind the house across the street." Alley Cat saw the horrified look on Black Cat's face and tried to explain. "Yes, it gets cold at night. But the Landlord won't let the People who live there have any pets. But the People have been pretty nice to me anyway. At least they don't chase me out of their yard like all the other People on this block do." Alley Cat's voice softened. "I really appreciate that."

"Black Cat!" Siamese Cat called again from the porch railing. Black Cat threw an anxious glance in her direction, but again her curiosity got the better of her.

"But wouldn't it be better to find some . . . well, better People to live with?"

"Better People? Sure, it would be nice to have a Family that dished out food three times a day!" Alley Cat gave a short laugh. "But who's going to adopt a cat as ugly as I am?"

Black Cat didn't know what to say.

"But," Alley Cat went on, "I'm not sure there are 'better' People than the People across the street. They have seven kids and barely enough food to go around the table—but they're sure to give some little scrap to me, and a kind word and a pat. Of course, those scraps don't help feed eight kittens, so. . . ."

". . . So you go around the neighborhood at night, trying to find food," Black Cat finished, a new look coming into her face.

"Why, yes," Alley Cat said, surprised. "How did you know?"

"Black Cat! Remember what I told you," Siamese Cat scolded crossly from her house.

Alley Cat sighed. "I guess I know how you know. I suppose you think that's awful."

Black Cat just stood there like she was thinking awfully hard.

Alley Cat looked embarrassed. "Well, I guess I'll go back across the street. But I want you to know that you have a very beautiful kitten."

"Wait!" Black Cat seemed hesitant. "Your kittens. Have you had very many?"

"Very many!" Alley Cat laughed. "This is my fifth litter—and that makes thirty-two children all together!"

Black Cat blinked, then grinned shyly. "This is just my first—six children in all. And I'm having a terrible time with the nap problem. Have you found any solutions with yours?"

"Oh my, yes! I . . ." then Alley Cat stopped. "Are you sure you want to stay and talk? I mean, your friend. . . ."

"Yes, I'm sure. No—wait. There's something else first. There's a place under my People's porch where an air vent from the furnace opens out. If you moved your kittens under there, they would surely be warm enough at night. C'mon, I'll show you."

"Black Cat!" screeched Siamese Cat.

"In a few minutes," Black Cat called back. "I have something important to do first." She picked up her kitten and led the way back up the sidewalk.

"Do you like cabbage?" Alley Cat asked, as the two cats trotted back toward Black Cat's house. Black Cat could only grunt because she had her kitten in her mouth. "Well, it tastes much better than it smells. I really have grown to like it—you'll have to come over and try it sometime. And wait'll you see my kittens. . . ."

Black Cat smiled to herself, as her new friend talked on and on.

"Be humble toward one another, always considering others better than yourselves" (Philippians 2:3b).

To the Parents

Prejudice is a big word for young children to comprehend—but prejudice begins at an early age. Young children often have a warm acceptance of all sorts of people, but this acceptance is easily influenced by the attitudes and reactions of others. Also, if a child feels insecure about his or her own identity or struggles with low self-esteem, he may try to build up his own importance by putting other people down.

After reading the story of Black Cat, Siamese Cat, and Alley Cat aloud to your child, you may want to use the following questions to discuss how we think about or relate to people who may look different or do things differently:

1. Why did Siamese Cat think she was so special?

2. Why didn't Siamese Cat like Alley Cat?

3. After listening to Siamese Cat, how do you think Black Cat felt about Alley Cat? Why?

4. What happened that helped change Black Cat's opinion of Alley Cat?

5. What did Black Cat learn about Alley Cat when she actually talked to her?

6. What did Black Cat and Alley Cat have in common?

7. What made Black Cat think Alley Cat could be a good friend, in spite of what Siamese Cat had said?

8. How did Black Cat offer to help Alley Cat? How did Black Cat ask Alley Cat to help her?

9. Do you think Black Cat can be friends with both Siamese Cat and Alley Cat? Why do you think so?